TALES OF THE UNCOOL

KINSLEY BOGGS
World Famous Naturalist

BY KIRSTEN RUE
ILLUSTRATED BY SARA RADKA

Kinsley Boggs: World Famous Naturalist
Tales of the Uncool

Copyright © 2015

Published by Scobre Educational

Written by Kirsten Rue

Illustrated by Sara Radka

Printed in the United States of America.

Scobre Educational
2255 Calle Clara
La Jolla, CA 92037

Scobre Operations & Administration
42982 Osgood Road
Fremont, CA 94539

www.scobre.com
info@scobre.com

Scobre Educational publications may be purchased for educational, business, or sales promotional use.

Cover and layout design by Jana Ramsay
Copyedited by Renae Reed

ISBN: 978-1-62920-143-6 (Soft Cover)
ISBN: 978-1-62920-142-9 (Library Bound)
ISBN: 978-1-62920-141-2 (eBook)

Table of Contents

Chapter 1	A New Friend	5
Chapter 2	Introductions	9
Chapter 3	Progress?	19
Chapter 4	The Kinsley Boggs Naturalist Tour	32
Chapter 5	We Will Prevail	44
Chapter 6	Bird Park	56

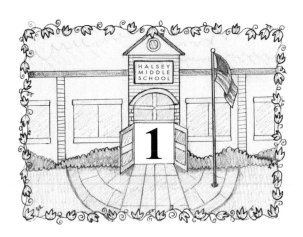

A New Friend

I WAS ON THE OUTER EDGE OF THE HALSEY SCHOOL yard looking for new flower shoots when I heard it: "CHICK-CHICK-BAWK!" I'm not going to lie to you: I just about jumped three feet in the air. I looked around but no one else was there. It was early, early spring and kinda starting to rain. I didn't have my good raincoat on or anything. Across the field, the Lardos were playing kickball and I was trying to stay as far away from *that* as possible. Near the Halsey doors—so far away they kinda looked like just a little drip of orange paint—most of the other kids stood in little circles, talking. Nobody explores like me. It's like they forget that there is this cool nature stuff ALL around, and not just in the summertime and not just when you plant it yourself.

Anyway, where was I . . . oh yeah, that CHICK-CHICK-BAWK! It was like nothing I'd ever heard. Not like any of the little songbirds that hop around our bird feeder. Not like the birds I've watched with my grandpa, using my own set of special binoculars. This was, like, LOUD. It was a BAWK! that, if you translated it, would probably say: "Kinsley Boggs! I need your attention right now, m'kay!"

And it HAD my attention. I love birds, slugs, panthers, Ruby (that's our three-legged golden retriever), gazelles, polar bears . . . everything! You name an animal, and I love it. I've maybe even read a *Young Naturalists* article about it. That's how much I love all animals. So, I kinda thought, wherever this bird was, he must have known that. He must have

known that I would want to help him. He could trust me.

A little flash of turquoise flashed by to my right. Vanished. Then, another flash, this time to my left! Vanished again. It was really starting to rain hard now, and I knew the recess bell was going to ring soon. I was getting kind of annoyed at this point.

"C'mon, bird. You have my attention, now where are ya?" I said. (This is one thing people don't really get about animals: Sure, they don't speak English, but you can *definitely* still communicate with them.)

Then, CHICK-CHICK-BAWK! A rolling feathery ball of turquoise and red and brown and beak came plunging at me from the edge of the fence. It rolled right up to me and then . . .

. . . It pooped on my shoe. I stared at him, and he stared back. He was plump and had feathers going all the way down to his claws. His breast was turquoise and red, and the colors on his face were a swirl of black and white. *Very* dramatic. He was small, but he looked pretty tough.

"Ewwwwww!!!" I screeched. And that, if you believe it, is how I first met Bob the Chinese Quail. Bob the Quail changed everything.

Introductions

EVERY MORNING WHEN I WAKE UP, I HAVE TO POKE Ruby, my dog, in the side before I can get out of bed. She usually makes a little whine (sometimes she even farts—gross!) and then that whine changes to a happy groan. She licks my face and hops down on her good front legs. Then, she scoots her butt and missing leg down at the same time. I hop down after her.

"Morning, Rubes!" That's how I know the day has started. Today is no different. I brush my teeth: twenty strokes on the left; twenty on the right. I give my mom a sloppy kiss on the cheek—extra sloppy on purpose so she'll make a pretend "Gross!" sound. Then I hop on the edge of the armchair where my grandpa is sitting, watching the bird feeders. That's his favorite thing: watching birds all day long. Like Mom always says, the two of us are peas in a pod.

"Hey, Grandad!"

He smiles at me, his blue eyes soft and peaceful. "Hey there, Chickadee! See who's visiting us today?" He points out at a little, bright yellow bird.

"I know it! It's a . . . a . . . goldfinch!"

"High five!" We slap palms and I go into the kitchen to make my lunch. Most of the other Halsey kids either eat the school lunch (don't ask me why, it's gross) or bring nice lunches from home. They have the crusts cut off their sandwiches and Diet Cokes and corn chips. I *guess* Mom would make me a lunch if I asked really nicely, but she knows I'm picky. "Picky eaters," she says, "can make their own lunches." So, I usually bring whatever sounds good to me that morning. Today, I'm in the mood for dill pickles, goldfish crackers, and some slices of fake chicken.

Oh, did I not tell you? I'm vegetarian. Have been since, like, forever. When you love animals like I do, you just kind of have to be.

I put everything in the lunch sack I sewed myself at camp over the summer—it has a print of brown bears on it. I sneak Ruby the crust of my mom's toast, and she gobbles it up in one bite. Then, I pour myself some cranberry juice in a thermos . . . AND, how could I almost forget?! I pack a little plastic baggie of bird pellets for Bob the Quail.

YOU DIDN'T THINK I'D FORGET ABOUT BOB, DID YOU? Bob is *expecting* me. We have a daily date, at least Monday through Friday. At 12:30 p.m. sharp, Bob will be waiting for me where I first discovered him. It's right up near the fence, where all the eighth graders throw their Freeburger cups (and where I pick them up). I think I get why Bob picked that spot. It's far away from the footballs getting thrown around, for one thing. He gets some peace and quiet. Also, there's a little clump of shrubs and a little pond—well, a big puddle—where he can dip his feet and drink. If I'm not there, I'm pretty sure he just hides in the shrubs.

According to Granddad, that's normal for a quail. Actually, it was Granddad who first helped me identify Bob the Quail. After I got over the shock of Bob "introducing" himself by pooping on my shoe, I took out my phone. Just before the recess bell rang, I snapped a picture of the bird and then splashed across the rainy field and back into school.

"Hmmmm," Grandad muttered, "hmmmm . . . verrrrry interesting. Now this is really something." He had put on his glasses and was squinting at the small photo on my hand-me-down phone. He compared it with various pages of his *Encyclopedia of North American Birds*. "Now, I'm pretty sure what we've got here is a quail, but the funny thing is, it doesn't seem to be from around here." Eventually, my mom brought her laptop down from upstairs and we started doing searches for "blue and red quail."

"Ah ha!" Granddad shouted in triumph. "I think we have a Chinese painted quail on our hands!"

"From China?!" I asked. I mean, that seemed like a long way to fly. And why come to our town? Or to Halsey?!

"Well," said Granddad, "It says here that these suckers are found in India, southeast China, and all over these tropical islands. Even near Australia!" He pointed at a map on the screen.

"Wooowww." I pictured the islands like New Guinea that I'd seen on some of my nature shows—jungles and bright parrots and blue-green water. Once again, I had to ask myself why the quail would trade all of that for Halsey. Not exactly a tropical retreat . . .

"You want to know my professional opinion?" Granddad asks. He never studied birds in school, but he does know a whole lot. Plus, he always likes to call things his "professional opinion," even if he's just telling me that I should wear a hat to school. "I think Bob might have been raised to be someone's pet. But somehow he got out."

"And now I need to take care of him!" I butted in.

"Well, I'm sure your quail could use a new friend."

"Bob," I said. "His name is Bob." I don't why, but the name just seemed perfect for the plump little bird I'd seen earlier that day.

"Bob definitely needs a friend," Granddad agreed.

———————

So, AT SCHOOL TODAY AT TWELVE-THIRTY, I WALK OVER TO the edge of the Halsey yard. There are a few more late February flowers poking out of the grass. That's good. Bob'll like that.

"*Chick-chick-bawk!*" I've been working on my quail call, but it's still pretty tough. I even put a special app on my phone so I can listen to the calls before I go to sleep at night. Being a naturalist takes a LOT of hard work. My heroes are people like Jane Goodall who have lived with apes in Africa, or people that try to preserve coral reefs. So, I guess what I'm saying is, yeah, a fat little blue quail isn't the most "glamorous" way to start. But why am I the first one to discover Bob? It has to be for a reason, and Bob *is* special. He needs my help. This is a good first step in my career.

After I call, Bob scuttles out from his favorite shrub. He looks up at me with his shiny black eyes. I squat down and spread some pellets on the ground. I've tried to pet him on his head, but he doesn't like that. I know Bob doesn't want me to treat him like a pet. He may have been raised to be one, but here's my opinion: Bob is a free quail and I should respect his independence. So I just leave some food for him and tell him about my day. Mrs. Pruggle has been *really* hard on us lately. So much homework, you wouldn't even believe! And Stella Sweet, the meanest and most popular girl in sixth grade, made fun of my lunch bag yesterday. I guess bear prints aren't her style.

Bob eats, and bobs his little head up to look at me. His red and turquoise feathers gleam. He makes a happy little chick-chick-chick sound.

"Alright, Bob. See you tomorrow!" With that, I head back across the field and Bob goes to stand in his puddle. As much as I like him, I also wish he could go home to where he's *really* from. I mean, does he get cold in this climate? Does he get lonely for other birds to hang out with? I feel bad that he has nothing but some scraggly shrubs, a puddle, and a sixth-grade girl to keep him company.

IN MS. ARPLE'S SCIENCE CLASS, MY FRIEND ESPERANZA sits next to me. Lately, though, she's been trying to get everyone to call her "Espere." I don't know. It sounds kind of fake to me. Esperanza has always been really good at drawing, so I bet she's trying to sound more *artistic*. Still, what's wrong with her regular name? Maybe I should change my name to Kin-SALA.

"Where do you *go* at recess?" Esperanza asks. "I know you do your 'walks' or whatever, but have you ever thought about *my* recess? I hate standing out there

all by myself." She makes a little frown at me.

That's one thing my mom always says: I don't always make enough of an effort to keep my friends. Last year, Esperanza and I talked a lot about having our own nature show someday. She's really good at science, though now she tells me she's more interested in the stars and planets. We called ourselves the Dynamic Duo and set up all kinds of experiments in Esperanza's big back yard. (Our back yard is tiny, so Ruby and I are always on the lookout for a good yard.) Then summer came around and I went to a camp far away where we spent all day tromping around the forest. That was AWESOME. By the time I came back, I sorta forgot about calling Esperanza. I was back in my own little world. But now that I think of it, Bob the Quail is just the kind of thing Esperanza would probably understand. She is my only science friend, after all. Plus, she can sketch.

"Tomorrow I'll take you there," I say.

We shake on it.

Progress?

EXCEPT, THE NEXT DAY WHEN ESPERANZA AND I are walking out over the fields, we notice something. Over there, in Bob the Quail's section of the Halsey Schoolyard, a crew of men with stakes and measuring lines are walking all over it. Bob the Quail is nowhere in sight. Have these men come to take him away? I break into a run.

"Hey! What are you doing over there?!" I shout at them. They turn.

"Kinsley!" Esperanza huffs from behind me. "Stop

running! My shoes are sticking in the mud! You're going to get us in trouble."

I cross the field so fast that I can feel flecks of mud splattering my jeans. Well, my naturalist heroes had to get dirty, too, right? All in a day's work. . . . I stop short in front of the men with their clipboards and plaid shirts. They all look at me like, *"Oh, great, now we have to deal with this weirdo kid."* Once I'm up closer, I notice that Mr. Speck the activities director is standing with them. Orange lines have been spray painted in the dirt in a square pattern.

"Excuse me," I say, but then I have to stop for a moment to catch my breath. It's not every day that I sprint straight across the whole Halsey field. "Excuse me," I say again, resting my hands on my knees. "Don't you know this is rare habitat of the endangered Chinese painted quail?"

"Huh?" All the workers stare at me.

"This is protected land," I continue. "It's a . . . a crucial, um—" *What's the word? What's the word?!—*

"watershed"—*Bingo!*—"for a quail that's already living here. And has been living here!"

Mr. Speck crosses his arms and looks annoyed. He's one of the youngest teachers at Halsey, but everyone says he plays favorites with the football Lardos. If you aren't good at sports, then don't even bother, they say. "A what-now?" he asks. "Who's living here?"

"His name is Bob," I tell him matter-of-factly. "Bob the Quail."

"Right." He glares. "Is this some kind of joke?"

Esperanza catches up to me and shoots me a warning glance.

"No, I'm serious." I say, keeping my voice calm, even though it sorta wants to shake. "I discovered a rare species of quail on this property and this is his home. He needs to be protected." I stick my chin up and throw my shoulders back, too. Just for good measure.

(So, sidenote: I'm not actually sure if the quail *is*

endangered or *is* supposed to be protected. I guess I'm kind of . . . stretching the truth? But it's for a good cause, I swear! I'm Bob's only friend in the world, and like it or not, Halsey is his home!)

Mr. Speck has muscly arms and a crease in his brow that's getting deeper the longer he has to talk to me. Esperanza reaches out and pinches my arm—I can feel it even underneath my coat sleeve.

"Ouch!" I elbow her back. Even though we haven't spent as much time together lately, I can still read her look one hundred percent. It says, "Kinsley Boggs, you are in BIG trouble."

Still, I can't stop myself. I even stomp my foot. "Mr. Speck, I have to demand that you stop whatever you're doing now!"

The workers with their measuring equipment stare at me. Esperanza stares at me with her mouth open. And Mr. Speck? I figure he's going to send me straight in to see Assistant Principal McCloud. I mean, you're not exactly allowed to yell at the teachers. But maybe because there are workers around or maybe just because he woke up on the right side of the bed, he doesn't.

"What's your name?" he asks me.

"Kinsley." I try hard not to stare at the crease between Mr. Speck's brows. I feel like somehow he'll be more annoyed at us if he catches me doing that.

"Well, Kinsley. We're building the new athletic equipment shed out here. I don't know what this thing about a bird is all about, but if you're concerned, you've gotta prove it." With that, he turns his back on me and strides back over to the others. "Ahem, gentlemen, I'm sorry for that little interruption," he says. He puffs out his chest. He actually reminds me of a bird when I really think about it. Like a goose strolling along the edge of a pond with his breast pushed out. Or a rooster, maybe.

I'm about to follow after him and try to explain even more, but Esperanza grabs my arm and starts dragging me back to the school. "Kinsley, we've got to GO! The bell's going to ring!"

"But, Bob! I didn't get to feed Bob!" I struggle to pull my arm away for a moment, and then Esperanza grabs my other arm and looks straight into my eyes. I've always liked her eyes. They're a coffee brown and it seems like she has little flecks of green in them, too. We're staring at each other, face to face.

"Look," Esperanza hisses at me. "I'm trying to HELP you. Maybe we can save this dale or Bob or kale or whatever. But NOT NOW."

"It's a QUAIL. Rhymes with 'jail.'" I feel just a teensy bit like crying in frustration. Usually I try to count to ten and take deep breaths to stop from crying, but this afternoon has been a lot to deal with. To top it off, Bob is probably hidden in his shrub, totally terrified right about now. He has no idea why his little corner of Halsey yard has suddenly been invaded. He didn't even get his lunch! It's all so unfair. But, Esperanza is taking this moment to continue to drag me towards the recess doors.

"Chop, chop," she says to me. "Get a move on."

We make it inside just as the bell begins to sound and she keeps pulling me towards science class. "Just keep moving," she says. "Don't get stuck." I guess that's kind of good advice. Poor Bob is stuck, and as I collapse into my desk in science class, I know there's gotta be something I can do to get him *un*-stuck.

AFTER CLASS, I TELL ESPERANZA TO WAIT FOR ME IN THE hall, and I go up to Ms. Arple.

"Ms. Arple," I ask. "Remember when we wrote practice letters to our Congresswoman about something we wish was different in the world?'

"Hmmm, yes, I think I do remember that," she says. She's also one of the younger teachers, and even though her voice is soft, she always seems to say interesting things. I think the little splash of freckles across her nose is especially cool. I have a little splash of freckles on my nose, too.

"Could I get the name and address of our Congresswoman again? Please?"

She goes over and flips open one of the bright binders she keeps on a big shelf next to all of her plants. Ms. Arple promised that we would study plants next month, and I'm pretty excited about that. After going through a few pages, she finds the one she needs and scribbles down the address for me on a Post-it note.

"Here ya go! Now go do your civic duty!" Ms. Arple laughs in kind of a dorky way. I realize that she's making a joke, so I laugh, too. I'm not sure I get it, though.

By the time I rejoin Esperanza in the hallway, I feel energized. My arms and legs are buzzing. I feel like I could shout or even do a handstand in the hall. (I am actually pretty good at handstands.) I know *exactly* what I'm going to do to save Bob.

THAT NIGHT, I FINISH MY HOMEWORK AND PULL A CHAIR up to my little desk in my little room. It looks over the yard, and I watch Ruby chase birds for a little bit. She never gets them, but they love to tease her. She does a little *hop hop hop* as she runs around on her three legs, trying to chomp one. I have my laptop open and the address from Ms. Arple. I have a blank document open on the computer. I want the letter to look official, after all. I already told Mom and Granddad at dinner about my plan to write to the Congresswoman.

"Good for you!" They said. "You tell 'em!"

Esperanza has told me before that my family goes a

little over the top with encouragement sometimes. She's probably right. I could say, "I'm going to go tie my shoe!" and they would reply, "Look at you go!"

Well, now, I'm ready to work. I stretch my arms above my head and rub my hands together. I crack my knuckles. I smell my hair, which I just washed. It smells like strawberries, the scent of my own special shampoo that I picked out myself. Okay, strawberry hair, rub hands, crack knuckles . . . let's go!

Dear Congresswoman Medina, **I begin.** I'm writing to you about a bird—

I get stuck at this point. I've never written a Congresswoman before. Not about something serious that affects an animal's life. The letters we wrote in class were just an exercise. This one is important, though. I picture it arriving at the Congresswoman's office in one, maybe two days. It will immediately be brought to her on a tray by one of her assistants. *How many assistants do you get?* I wonder. "Let's get started on this!" she'll say, as soon as she's read it. "Call the principal of this Halsey School. Call the president. We need new legislation. And call this brave girl—Kinsley Boggs. I'd like to thank her personally." *Hmmm.* . . . I mean, I'm not sure if it will go exactly like that, but Bob's home will probably be saved within a few days, right?

I know that now, I need to act like one of my conservation heroes. I have to write people and give interviews and get my picture in the paper. I'm exhausted just thinking about it. This letter is the first step in all of that, but still, I can't seem to get beyond "I'm writing to you about a bird." I need some help. I pull out my phone and search for Esperanza's number.

"Hello?"

It's Esperanza's little brother, and when I ask for her by name, he screams, "Espere, someone's calling you!" back into their house. I'm surprised she has convinced her whole family to call her Espere instead of Esperanza. Don't they feel, I dunno . . . kinda offended? They did give her the name, after all.

"Ugh, Eric, you are so annoying," I can hear her say. "Hello?"

"Hey, Esperanza . . ." After she gets over the shock of me calling her at home, I explain to her that I need help with this letter. I don't know the right way to save Bob, not really. How can we stop that athletic shed from being built right on top of his home? I'm putting my hope in this letter, and I've got to get it in the mail as soon as possible.

"Well . . ." Esperanza says, thinking on the other line. I can hear her clicking her fingernails against the phone's receiver. "I don't know if it's going to be as fast as you think."

"Really?" my heart sinks.

"Yeah, well, I don't know if this is true or not, but my dad says that they don't even write you back themselves."

"Why not?"

"Because their desks are piled *high* with letters from all over the country. They have other people write you back."

"Yeah, but THIS letter is important."

"How're they gonna know that? I mean, to her and her workers, envelopes just look like envelopes."

I sigh. That's a good point, I have to admit.

"Why are you going straight to a Congresswoman anyway? I bet there's a faster way. Why not ask someone who's actually from our town, or Halsey?"

"Good idea!" Why didn't *I* think of that?

"Why not share this special bird, if he is so special? So far, you're like the only person who's even seen him." *Another* good idea. Man, Esperanza is on a roll! I'm relieved that I called her—she always has good advice. I need to call her more often. Bonus: this means I don't have to keep writing that boring old letter. I can do something more *unique* instead.

"Okay!" I agree, but when we hang up, I have to admit, I still feel stuck. What *unique* thing should I do? How can I get the rest of the school to care about Bob?

The Kinsley Boggs Naturalist Tour

THE NEXT MORNING, DURING THE IN-BETWEEN MINUTES *after* I poke Ruby in the side to wake her up and *before* she starts licking my face, I think about the nature shows that I love. More than anything, they made me care about the forest and animals I've never seen in real life. It's not like I even thought much about birds before Granddad moved in with us. Before, they were just those creatures you saw flying overhead, or the little birdies that jumped out of the way as you walked on the sidewalks. But now? Now that I've watched birds with Granddad and read my science magazines and watched my nature shows? Now, I feel like I can picture birds, all over the world. I can picture them, and I care about what happens to them. Maybe that's what Bob needs. Maybe he needs to be *visible* to everybody, just like Esperanza said.

With my eyes still kind of tired from sleep and Ruby just starting to lick my chin, I pull my phone out from underneath my pillow.

"I'm not really supposed to talk on the phone on school mornings," Esperanza whispers to me once she answers. "I'm supposed to be getting ready."

"I know, I know, I just wanted to ask you one thing. Can you sketch a picture of Bob for me?"

"Um, sure," she says, after a pause. "Geez, Kinz, most of the other girls at Halsey probably call each other about boys or lip-gloss or something. But you?"

"I'm calling about a bird. I know. Not very cool."

Esperanza laughs. "Just don't call me in the morning! I like to sleep in!"

THAT DAY AT RECESS, I INTRODUCE BOB AND ESPERANZA. When we approach his habitat, I don't see him. My heart starts pounding with fear that he was scared away by the workers yesterday, or worse . . . maybe he got hurt or confused and is wandering around somewhere dangerous. I hope he didn't try to fly over the fence or cross the road! Quails can fly, my Granddad said, but they also like to return to where they're comfortable. In this neighborhood, Bob doesn't fit in (kind of like me)—it's not a safe place for him. When we reach his section of Halsey yard, I take a deep breath and pull back some of the branches of his favorite shrub.

I see a chubby little turquoise and red bird. *Phew!*

"Bob, I'm so glad you're still here!" I reach in and stroke one of his feathers. When he comes out to eat his lunch, I let Esperanza feed him instead of me.

"Here, birdie birdie birdie!" she calls. "Hi, Bob!" Bob seems to approve, and luckily, he doesn't poop on her shoe. He waddles around the edge of his little puddle, making his satisfied chick-chick-chick sound.

"He really is kind of cute," Esperanza says. She has her sketchbook out and is flicking her eyes back and forth between Bob and the page. Her pencil is flying.

While she sketches, I walk around the area that Bob calls home. The orange spray paint lines from the other day are still there on the grass. I can see footprints where workers have been walking around, probably right THROUGH Bob's pond. I shake my head. This is *not* acceptable. Who needs an athletic equipment shed, anyway? Why not get more plants for Ms. Arple's room or more paperbacks for the library? Why do we need a bunch of stupid sports stuff taking up a whole precious corner of Halsey lawn? Now the Lardos will be everywhere: throwing footballs, playing tetherball. It's not just Bob that'll be affected. All of the little flowers will be squashed. Butterflies and bees will stay away in the springtime. Nature will be *ruined*.

"Done!" Esperanza shouts. I've been brooding

so much about the Halsey yard being invaded that I almost forgot she was here. "Let's go!"

"Bye, Bob!" We call over our shoulders. "Don't let those guys bother you! We're going to help you out!"

ESPERANZA SLIDES HER SKETCH OVER TO ME DURING science class, and I have to say, it looks pretty good. Sure, Bob's neck looks a little short and right now it's just in black-and-white, but I dunno. It does kinda capture his "CHICK-CHICK-BAWK!" expression and his skinny little feet. She colors the portrait in during free period and hands it off to me right before we board our separate buses. I give her a thumbs-up sign. Only after boarding the bus do I notice that she's written SAVE BOB! in big letters right over his head. That makes me laugh for sure.

BY THE NEXT MORNING, I'VE GOT ONE HUNDRED FLIERS copied with Esperanza's sketch and these words written at the bottom: Come meet Bob! Halsey

School's endangered species. Tours led at 12:30 after lunch. Meet at flagpole. Extra credit!! I made Mom drive me instead of the taking the bus so I could stop at a copy shop before school. I even used all the money I had been saving for this summer's forest camp to make the copies!

And, um, I did lie, just a *teensy* bit about the whole extra credit thing. Also, Bob's not endangered in the *legal* sense of the word. He's more just . . . lonely. But, hey, I've gotta get people to come see him, right? It's like my mom always says, "Be *aware*." She's usually talking about being aware about cars coming or how much homework I have to finish before TV time. But, this is awareness, too. Halsey School is going to realize that they've got a special creature living on the lawn, and that they shouldn't scare him away with a shed. Or hockey sticks. Or tennis rackets.

I LEAVE THE CAFETERIA EARLY SO THAT I CAN GET TO the flagpole in time. While I stand there, I stick on a nametag sticker with Kinsley Boggs written on it. I know that most of the kids at Halsey don't even know my name. I'm just that uncool. I'm also holding up one of my fliers. I cross my fingers and try to cross my toes inside my shoes, but my socks kinda get in the way. I squinch my eyes close. *Please, let Bob get saved.* When I open them, a couple of other students are standing there. Joe Russo, one of the Lardos, Dana, one of the Sweets, Tina, and Julian. See. I know all of *their* names.

"Um . . . extra credit?" Joe asks. He could probably use some for sure.

"Yep!" I say brightly, "Right this way!" I walk fast and with energy, just like the hosts of the nature shows I watch. I figure I should make my tour as informative as possible, so I add some stuff along the way. "To your right you'll see a scarlet oak tree. And that, that plant you just stepped on, Joe, is a dead milk thistle." The other students don't say anything, but I *do* hear Dana the Sweet saying, "Ewwww! I'm getting water all over my shoes!" Of course, I *wish* Esperanza could be here for moral support, but she has a dentist appointment right this very second.

When I arrive at Bob's corner of the yard, I feel a little too embarrassed to do my quail call. I've never practiced it in front of people before, and I'm afraid it might come out more like a "Squawk!" Who knows, maybe that will even scare Bob away. So, I tell everyone else to keep back and hold one finger to my lips. "Shhhhh," I say. "Be very still." Tina rolls her eyes at Julian, but I pretend not to notice. I go up to Bob's shrub and spread his pellets out on the ground. There's a rustle, and then he pokes his head out from the shrub. His black and white face looks as amazing as ever. I spread some more food, and he walks out, pecking and beginning to make his happy sound. For what it's worth, the other kids don't say a word.

"*This* . . . is Bob." I turn around and smile. Like, *ta da!* Bob notices the other kids, but maybe after having so many workmen tramping around his turf, he doesn't seem to mind. He just pecks at his food and scuttles from place to place. The sun breaks through the clouds overhead and I swear it shines directly on Bob's red and turquoise feathers. I don't know, though. I can't tell if the other kids are impressed or not. They're just standing there, staring at me. I have a whole speech prepared, and I figure I better dive in before I lose my audience. It isn't really like I planned when I thought it all through in my bedroom last night, though.

"Um-this-is-Bob-he's-a-rare-Chinese-um-painted-quail-and-um-that's-a-bird-you-don't-see-in-our-town-because-er-they're-from-Asia-and-it's-a-mystery-how-he-got-here-but-Mr.-Speck-is-building-an-athletic-shed-right-on-top-of-his-house-and-we-have-to-stop-him!"

With that, I hold out my clipboard and the petition I've created. I mean, I stayed up *really* late writing this thing and preparing for the tour.

Stop Halsey School From Building On Animal Habitat is its title. I've even made a space for one hundred signatures below. Aim high, right?

However, the other kids don't seem to be getting it.

"What's that?" whines Dana. "Is that how we get our extra credit?"

"Why are you saying bad stuff about Mr. Speck?!" asks Joe Russo, his cheeks coloring red.

"Is this all . . . a trick?" asks Julian, a guy I've always kinda liked, even if he doesn't know me.

"No! I'm trying to make people aware. Trying to save this bird." I gesture back to Bob, who is still pecking at his food. *I* still think he looks beautiful and exotic. But I can see it from the other kids' point of view: A girl they don't know promised them extra credit. She made them walk across a wet field. She showed them a small bird that just stood there eating food, not really doing anything. She said a speech, so fast they couldn't even hear her—not really. And then she shoved a clipboard in their faces and asked them to sign. I guess I *did* kind of trick them.

I hang my head. This is not at all how I wanted

things to play out.

"Ugh, what a waste of time! Kinsley—if that's even your *real* name—you are a NERD!" says Dana, flouncing away. Joe follows her, muttering, "I'm going to tell Mr. Speck on you," as he goes. They both turn their heads a couple of times to glare at me.

That leaves Tina and Julian, and only Julian signs the petition. I think he feels bad for me. Tina won't even sign. She crosses her arms and looks away. After that, they shake their heads and walk back across the field. I catch the words *"So* weird!" I'm sure they're talking about me. *Sigh.* Now I'm alone with Bob. You'd think he'd show some kind of gratitude considering all the work I'm doing to save his home. Right now this whole thing almost doesn't feel worth it.

The first Kinsley Boggs Naturalist Tour? *A total failure.*

We Will Prevail

"**I**'M TOO DEPRESSED TO GO TO SCHOOL TODAY," I SAY to Esperanza on the phone the next day.

"Kinz, I wish you would stop calling in the mornings. My mom *hates* that!"

"Sorry. Ugh. I wish you could have been there yesterday. I made a TOTAL fool of myself. I even annoyed that nice Julian guy."

"Nice Julian? Man, he's usually so . . . well, *nice.*"

"I guess he did sign . . ."

"So, that's good! You have one signature!"

"No, that sucks," I correct Esperanza, glumly. "I'm going to lie and say we have today off. My Granddad won't care and Mom's already at work this morning." Beside me on the bed, Ruby starts thumping her tail. She obviously wants me to stay home all day, too.

"Well, but haven't you heard?" Esperanza asks. "I think today is the day they're going to start digging the hole for the new athletic shed."

"Wait, WHAT?!" I sit straight up in bed.

"Yeah, my dad knows some people who are working on it. He told me this morning."

"Espere? I have to go!" I yell, jumping out of bed and starting to search one-handed for jeans on my bedroom floor. Ruby jumps down, too, and begins to bark at me.

"Hey, you finally called me 'Espere!'" Esperanza says happily.

"Don't get too excited. I'm just in a hurry." I hang up.

I have to sprint to make the bus, so I don't even get

a chance to pack my lunch bag. Not that I'm craving anything special. Not even a dill pickle. I didn't bring my book bag, either, because you know what? I have no intention of going to class today. Nope. As soon as the bus drops me off at the front of the school, I march straight towards the Halsey yard, cross it, and lie down in front of Bob's shrub. Bob is there, resting peacefully inside the thick branches. I lie down right over the spot where the workmen are going to come and dig their hole.

Of course, as soon as I lie down, I wish I'd planned a little better. For one thing, I forgot to put socks on. For another, it sure would be nice to have something like a tarp to separate me from the wet grass. And the last thing? I forgot to bring any signs or even my petition to explain about why Halsey School needs to save Bob. This is going to be a looonnggg day. I can't move, though, because that would defeat the purpose of my sit-in. For a sit-in, you actually have to, ya know, *sit*. Once you stand up, it means you've given up. For the first hour or two, nobody comes to bother me. Even Bob seems bored. He just sits under his shrub and gives the occasional chick-chick-chick. I wish Esperanza had a cellphone so I could at least text her. That's another thing I forgot to do: tell a single person that I'm protesting today.

I check my watch. 10:30. Finally, I start to see some people walking across the field towards me. Then, I hear a rumbling, and a small dumptruck pulls up to the curb on the other side of the fence behind me. I've been sitting up, but now I lie back down. I squint into the shrub at Bob. "I hope you appreciate this, Bob." Bob stares back at me. I think he's probably just wondering why I've been here so long without feeding him a single bite. The workmen approach, and the dumptruck's engine rumbles from just beyond the gate.

Finally, they arrive. A group of three holding shovels.

"Stop!" I call out.

They all look around, confused, before they see me

lying on the grass directly on the spot where the new shed is supposed to go.

"I am having a sit-in. To protect a rare bird that lives here."

"Hey, that's the little girl from the other day!" says one of the workers. He must have been one of the men out there with Mr. Speck. *Grrrr, "little,"* I think to myself. Don't even try to stop me, Buster.

"Look, kid. We're just hired to do a job here. Could you just move for a second so we can get started? You can pick up your bird or whatever."

"Shouldn't you be in school anyway?" says another one of the workmen.

I just keep lying on the grass and bring my eyebrows together in the most serious scowl I can manage. "I'm not moving until the shed is moved to another section of Halsey yard," I say in my firm voice. I try to sound like a detective from a cop show on TV or something. *Very serious and very low and very "don't mess with me."*

"Man, you've got to be kidding me!" The first workman says. "I hate this job sometimes." He pulls out a walkie-talkie from his belt loop. "Yeah, we've got a situation here," he says into its crackly-sounding mouthpiece. "There's a girl lying down on the grass and she won't move."

NOW, I DON'T EXACTLY KNOW HOW THAT MESSAGE INTO the walkie-talkie could pass through the whole school in less than an hour, but it does. Mr. Speck jogs out onto the field, the crease between his eyebrows as dark as a canyon. Assistant Principal McCloud comes out (though he doesn't jog). Ms. Arple, my science teacher, comes out, looking pretty confused. I've got a whole ring of teachers staring at me and a whole ring of workmen. And they look MAD.

But then, guess who crosses the field, too?

Esperanza. I see her slip out a side door and bolt towards me. She sits down right on the other side of Bob's favorite shrub.

"I can't believe you're doing this!" she whispers to me.

"Now, what is going on here?" Mr. Speck says in annoyance. "Morty, can you do anything?" (Morty is the assistant principal's first name.)

"We are not going to move until the endangered bird that lives on this spot is protected!" Esperanza says, loud enough for the whole group to hear.

"Will one of you call their parents? Can we get this taken care of, NOW?!" Mr. Speck asks. He's shifting his weight back and forth and back and forth. Almost like he really has to pee or something. I think he just can't wait for us to be peeled off the ground so they can start construction on his shed. I mean, seriously dude, it's just a shed!

"I will, I will," Assistant Principal McCloud says, hurrying back towards the school.

Esperanza whispers to me again. "Do you have a chant or anything that you can say? I feel like at these sit-in thingies, they always have a chant to say." Man,

Esperanza is a lot more into this conservation stuff than I thought. We really *are* the Dynamic Duo.

"Um, give me a sec. . . . What about, 'Save the Quail! We will prevail!' I think that means we'll win. Or something close."

"Save the quail! We will prevail!" she begins to chant, and I join her. We try to shout as loudly as we can. To tell the truth, I want our words to echo all the way over to the rest of the Halsey sixth graders. I can see them coming outside for recess from across the field. Now's my chance to get their support, or at least attention. I know that I pretty much screwed up my tour of Bob's habitat and I *double* screwed up my petition. Still, how can they not see it's a good cause? This is their yard, too, after all. I know guys like Joe Russo want every square foot of Halsey to be somehow related to sports, but what about the rest of us? We want to be able to smell the grass and pick a dandelion or two. We want to see wild animals. We want nature to stick around! *This* is exactly why I want to be a conservationist. I want everyone in the world to know about what's beautiful around them, and be able to enjoy it in the way they like best. I want other people to get to see all the incredible plants and animals that I see. I mean, nature doesn't belong to one person, right? We all get to have it. We've got to make sure that people building buildings and roads don't build right over what belongs to everybody.

Assistant Principal McCloud is now hurrying back across the field towards us again. I guess that means he's called both of our parents. It's hard for me to predict how my mom will react to the news, but one thing I *do* know? She is going to be very mad about getting pulled from a busy shift at the hospital to come deal with me.

"Man, my parents are going to *kill* me," Esperanza says, looking down.

"I totally won't hold it against you if you stand up now!" I reply. "Honest. You don't have to get in trouble for me."

Esperanza shakes her head, her ponytail flapping back and forth behind her head. "No offense, but it's not really about you. It's about Bob." I hear Bob make one of his happy noises. He's sitting right at Esperanza's feet. Almost like he can understand us! Now, another figure is walking very, very slowly to join our small chanting group, the teachers standing around drinking coffee and looking mad, and the workmen also drinking coffee and looking mad. No . . . it couldn't be!

It's Granddad. I have no idea how he got a car to drive or paid for a cab, but he's HERE. Right in front of me. He's wearing his Irish-style driving cap and carrying the smooth-topped cane he likes to carry around town. I haven't seen him away from his bird-watching chair in the daytime very often. Yet as he walks now, he looks pretty healthy.

"Ah, Mr. Boggs," Assistant Principal McCloud says, holding out his hand. "I believe this is your granddaughter?"

"That is correct," Granddad says with a nod, but instead of stopping and shaking hands, he keeps walking.

"Have room for a third?" he asks Esperanza and me.

I throw my arms around his neck. Slowly, being careful not to strain his back, Granddad sits down on my other side.

"Now, what's this we're saying?" he asks. "Something about 'we will prevail?'"

"Granddad, are you sure you want to do this? I'm in so much trouble!" I say.

"And I couldn't be prouder of you," he says back, smiling his crinkly smile.

Bird Park

THE OTHER ADULTS STARE AT GRANDDAD. I CAN TELL they aren't quite sure what to do. Can I tell you something? It's not like I wanted to cause everybody a lot of trouble. I mean, I know they are just finding out about Bob. (Bob is now sitting right next to Granddad's knee. He definitely knows a bird lover when he meets one.) The workmen and the teachers don't want to build over his home, or at least, they didn't decide to build that shed over his home on purpose. BUT, if I wasn't here, if I WASN'T kinda being a pain, there would be a big hole where we are sitting now. I feel happy because, well, I am really doing it! I am being just like one of the naturalists I admire. In fact—and this thought makes my chest swell up like a balloon—I *am* one.

Esperanza and I grin at each other. The students I hoped would see us, from recess, begin trickling over. The sixth graders know when there's good gossip happening and *no one* wants to miss it. I am sort of counting on that. Just then a lady tiptoes over the grass towards us wearing a nice suit. She's followed by a man with a video camera. IT'S CLARISSA RECKENBECK FROM CHANNEL 4! I can hardly believe it! When Clarissa nears all of the commotion, she turns towards the camera and clears her throat.

"We're standing here at Halsey Middle School, where a student has decided to stage a sit-in," she says to the camera.

"Wow! Cool!" Esperanza says to me. We squeal and squeeze each other's hands. On my Top Five

Coolest Days Ever, I think today is number one.

At this point, the workmen shake their heads, grab their tools, and leave. They must not want to be on TV. Mr. Speck storms back to the school. As he goes, he waves his arms at the students who are coming to watch, shouting, "Nothing to see here! Nothing at all!"

Ms. Arple and the assistant principal whisper to one another. I think they are making a plan.

Clarissa Reckenbeck walks around the side of Bob's pond and approaches us.

"Gosh, I should have worn rain boots today," she says with a laugh, bending over where we're sitting. "Now who organized this sit-in to protect a bird?" she asks, holding out her microphone.

At first I can barely speak. I mean, this is Clarissa Reckenbeck from TV I'm staring at! Her hair is even shinier and her teeth even whiter in person. But then I remember that this is what it's all about. *This* is my chance to get attention for Bob. I clear my throat. "Um, I did," I speak up, as loudly as I can. Is this really happening?! "It's about a bird who's living here. I—I named him Bob."

"What about Bob?" she asks in a serious voice. I am *impressed*. Clarissa Reckenbeck's serious voice is exactly like the one I've been trying to practice for months now.

"Well, he's a Chinese painted quail. Far from home and very special. And this is where he's been living. In Halsey yard. I just want the other students to be able to enjoy this stuff. The nature that's here. And maybe the athletic equipment shed could go somewhere else?"

The cameraman points his camera at Bob.

"I think you must be very brave," Clarissa says. We're still on camera. "Who's here with you today?"

"My Granddad and my best friend." I smile.

So much happens after that: my mom comes to pick us up. Esperanza's mom comes, looking worried. Mr. Speck stalks back out to the field to make more plans with Assistant Principal McCloud. And finally, I am home in my room, lying quietly with Ruby beside me. "What do you think will happen?" I ask her. Ruby just gives me a look like, "*Duh*, I'm a dog. I can't help you with that." Am I worried that I'm in BIG trouble? Well, a little. Mostly, I'm worried for Esperanza. Mom even said in the car, "Look, Kinsley, I know these kinds of things are your dream, but what about your friend?" I get it. She has a point. Truthfully, I never told Esperanza about my plans, though. When I finally fall asleep, I have a series of dreams. In some of them, Bob is living in happiness on a tropical island, surrounded by fruit trees. In another, I come across Esperanza in front of her locker, crying.

"Now I'll never get to study the stars and planets!" she moans in the dream. "They're kicking me out of school!"

Yeah, that dream sucks.

THE NEXT DAY I GO WITH MY MOM AND GRANDDAD TO meet with the assistant principal and Mr. Speck. When we sit across the table from them, Mr. McCloud slides a piece of paper across the desk at me. It's one of my petition pages, except this time, it actually has names on it. Like, a LOT of names.

"Do you know anything about this?" he asks me.

"Yes," I say, looking down. "That's my petition to protect Bob—I mean the Chinese painted quail's—habitat."

"I see," he says, folding his fingers together and rocking back in his chair. "It seems that your little . . . *show* yesterday got some people's attention." *Good!* I think to myself.

"I've been talking with Mr. Speck and your science teacher, and we've decided on a new plan. We're going to build the athletic equipment shed behind the gym instead."

Yes! I pump my fist under the table.

"And YOU will be in charge of maintaining the Halsey School Rare Bird Garden."

"Is that—is that its name?" I can hardly believe it!

But before I jump up to do a little jig of happiness next to McCloud's desk, I think of my friend.

"What about my friend? Esperanza. None of this was her idea. I don't want her to be in trouble."

"Well, you BOTH need to make up the work you missed yesterday," McCloud says sternly. "But, we at Halsey School can't have news cameras around. That's the *last* thing we need for the school to run smoothly. So. If you can maintain your park, I'm ready to forget about the whole thing." I'm already turning to Granddad with a huge grin of triumph when McCloud adds, "But DON'T make this kind of thing a habit. You hear?"

"No, I won't! I promise!" I notice that the assistant principal has his own pretty goldfish in a bowl on his desk. Maybe he understands about nature after all.

———

"YOU WERE LUCKY," MOM SAYS AS SHE AND GRANDDAD put their coats back on. "I hope you'll think about what the man said. Not *everything* is a protest."

"Sure, sure," I say, squeezing Granddad's soft hand. His eyes shine back at me.

As I rush towards my locker, hoping to find Esperanza and hear her side of the story, my mind fills with ideas. I'll have a bench right next to Bob's pond, and I'll plant tulips and maybe even a rhododendron bush. Anyone will be welcome to come and sit in the garden. You'll be able to read on the bench, or lie back on the grass and look at the sky. I'll line Bob's pond

THE HALSEY SCHOOL
RARE BIRD GARDEN

HOME OF A BELOVED
CHINESE PAINTED QUAIL

with pretty stones. I can have Granddad help me. And, I'll have a plaque, too. Yes! Right next to the bench. Shiny and made out of stainless steel or some other fancy material. It will say:

THE HALSEY SCHOOL RARE BIRD GARDEN: HOME OF A BELOVED CHINESE PAINTED QUAIL